The Elves
and the
Shoemaker

by Amelia Marshall and Elena Bia

W
FRANKLIN WATTS
LONDON•SYDNEY

Many years ago there lived a shoemaker and his wife. They were good people and they worked hard. But they were very poor.

One day, the shoemaker had just

enough leather left for one pair of shoes.

The shoemaker cut the leather into pieces.
Then he left the pieces on his bench
and went to bed. In the morning
he would make the leather into shoes.

The next day, there was a pair of perfect shoes on his workbench.

The shoemaker's wife put the shoes
in the shop window.

Soon, a man came in to try on the shoes.
He liked them so much that he paid more
money than the price of the shoes.

The shoemaker bought enough leather
to make two pairs of shoes.

Once again, the shoemaker cut
the leather into pieces.
Then he left the pieces on his bench
and went to bed. In the morning,
he would make the leather into shoes.

The next day, there were two pairs
of perfect shoes on his workbench.
"We will be able to sell these for a lot
of money," said the shoemaker.
"It will be enough money for lots more
leather," said the shoemaker's wife.

The shoemaker's wife put the shoes in the window. People came to look at them. Soon, both pairs of shoes had been sold.

This time, the shoemaker had enough money to buy leather for four pairs of shoes.

Again, the shoemaker cut the leather with his scissors. Then he put the pieces on his bench. But he did not go up to bed.

"Let's stay up and see who has been helping us," he said to his wife. So, the shoemaker and his wife hid behind the curtains.

At midnight, two tiny elves came into the shop. They were dressed in rags and had no shoes on their feet.

The elves started to work.
They stitched and sewed, they cut
and trimmed. Soon, the shoes were
finished and the elves were gone.

The next day, the shoemaker sold
four pairs of shoes.

"Those elves are making us rich," he said.

"We must do something to thank them."

"I can make clothes to keep them warm,"
said his wife.

"Then I will make shoes for their feet,"
said the shoemaker.

That night, the elves found the shoes
and the clothes lying on the workbench.
They put them on and danced around.
They danced across the floor
and out through the door.

The shoemaker and his wife never saw
the elves again.

And they were never poor again.

Story order

Look at these 5 pictures and captions.
Put the pictures in the right order
to retell the story.

1

Two little elves make more shoes.

2

A man buys the new shoes.

3

The elves find the new clothes.

4

A new pair of shoes appears in the morning.

5

The shoemaker goes to bed.

Independent Reading

This series is designed to provide an opportunity for your child to read on their own. These notes are written for you to help your child choose a book and to read it independently.

In school, your child's teacher will often be using reading books which have been banded to support the process of learning to read. Use the book band colour your child is reading in school to help you make a good choice. *The Elves and the Shoemaker* is a good choice for children reading at Purple Band in their classroom to read independently.

The aim of independent reading is to read this book with ease, so that your child enjoys the story and relates it to their own experiences.

About the book

The shoemaker and his wife discover some little helpers are making shoes while they sleep. With the money from selling the new shoes, the shoemaker and his wife make the elves some shoes of their own!

Before reading

Help your child to learn how to make good choices by asking: "Why did you choose this book? Why do you think you will enjoy it?" Look at the cover together and ask: "What do you think the story will be about?" Ask your child to think of what they already know about the story context. Then ask your child to read the title aloud. Ask: "What do you think the elves are doing? What do you know about elves?"

Remind your child that they can sound out the letters to make a word if they get stuck.

Decide together whether your child will read the story independently or read it aloud to you.

During reading

Remind your child of what they know and what they can do independently. If reading aloud, support your child if they hesitate or ask for help by telling the word. If reading to themselves, remind your child that they can come and ask for your help if stuck.

After reading

Support comprehension by asking your child to tell you about the story. Use the story order puzzle to encourage your child to retell the story in the right sequence, in their own words. The correct sequence can be found on the next page.

Help your child think about the messages in the book that go beyond the story and ask: "Why do you think the elves make the shoes in the night time? Why do the shoemaker and his wife make something for the elves in return?"

Give your child a chance to respond to the story: "What was your favourite part and why? How would you describe the shoemaker and his wife?"

Extending learning

Help your child understand the story structure by using the same sentence patterning and adding different elements. "Let's make up a new story about the elves. Who might they help this time? What could they make? What might be their reward?"

In the classroom, your child's teacher may be teaching different kinds of sentences. There are many examples in this book that you could look at with your child, including statements, commands and questions. Find these together and point out how the end punctuation can help us decide what kind of sentence it is.

Franklin Watts
First published in Great Britain in 2022
by The Watts Publishing Group

Series Editors: Jackie Hamley and Melanie Palmer
Series Advisors and Development Editors: Dr Sue Bodman and Glen Franklin
Series Designers: Peter Scoulding and Cathryn Gilbert

A CIP catalogue record for this book is
available from the British Library.

ISBN 978 1 4451 8411 1 (hbk)
ISBN 978 1 4451 8412 8 (pbk)
ISBN 978 1 4451 8473 9 (library ebook)
ISBN 978 1 4451 8472 2 (ebook)

Printed in China

Franklin Watts
An imprint of
Hachette Children's Group
Part of The Watts Publishing Group
Carmelite House
50 Victoria Embankment
London EC4Y 0DZ

An Hachette UK Company
www.hachette.co.uk

www.reading-champion.co.uk

FSC
www.fsc.org
MIX
Paper from
responsible sources
FSC® C104740

Answer to Story order: 4, 2, 5, 1, 3